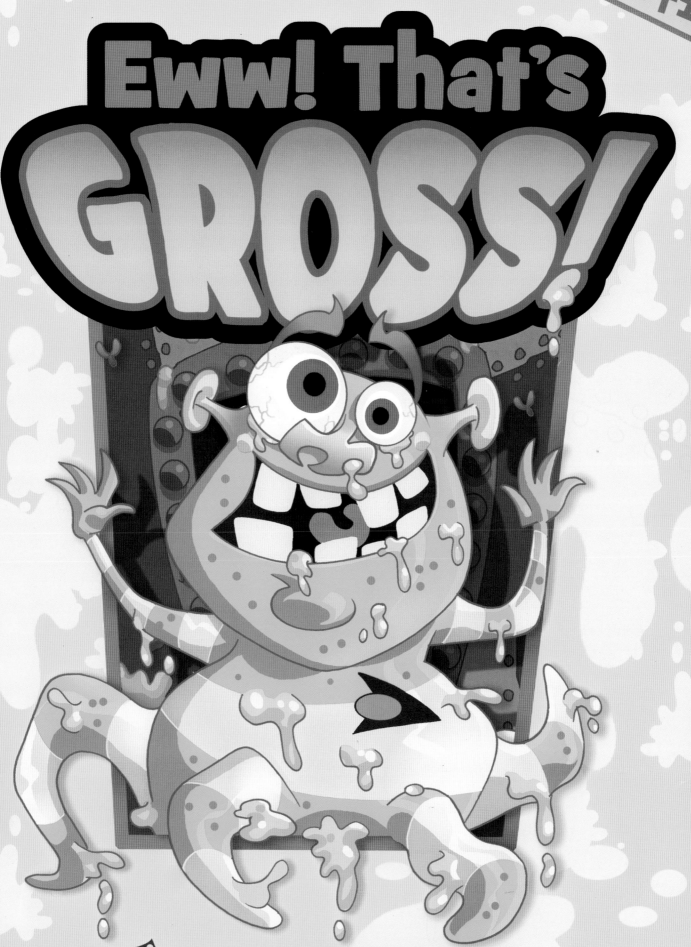

Eww! That's GROSS!

pi kids®

publications international, ltd.

Hi! I'm Commander Boog. Welcome to Planet Blech, a place where gooey goop fills every plate and moldy mucus is the planetary drink. Soon I'll travel to Earth to find a human who shares our love for the dreadful and disgusting. Can you find these members of my space crew?

Private Pimpler

Private Fartington

Lieutenant Slime

Captain Scabs

Sergeant Stinkers

Corporal Muck

GARBAGE DELIVERY

BOOGER KING

GROSSERY STAND

ICE SCREAMS

All aboard! welcome to our spaceship, the G.S.S. yechh. we've loaded it with all the comforts of home. I just can't wait to find an ugh-worthy human to study. That reminds me, it's time to refuel the engine with more pimple juice! Find these luxuries and games onboard the ship.

Squashed beetle chandelier

Stinky feet massage chair

Puke punch

Scabbers Board Game

Plungerboard Stick

Armpit sweat bath

Snotty nose painting

We've finally landed at an Earthling city dump. Our spaceship will be nicely hidden among this gooey, gruesome garbage. After we hide our spaceship, we're heading off to find the grossest human around. Can you find some of this gross Earth garbage?

Chunky milk

Rotten fish

Dentures

Refrigerator

Old toilet

Bedpan

CITY DUMP

We've heard rumors that the grossest Earth being is called a "human boy." So here we are, in a boys' locker room. What we heard is true — these human boys are truly disgusting, even by Planet Blech standards. Find these signs of boys' grossness.

Snotty tissues

This moldy Showerhead

Slimy Sweatbands

This locker

Flypaper

Moldy Sports drink

Overflowed toilet

Jockstrap

we've finally introduced ourselves. Chip seemed a little surprised to have aliens in his bedroom, but he'll get used to it! we plan on staying for a few months for our research. Can you find these things that make us feel right at home?

Toenail clippings

worms

Dirty cotton swabs

Moldy slice of pizza

Slug

Fake vomit

Basket of Dirty Socks

It's great living with Chip. Today he is throwing a party to welcome us to Earth. Can you find these children having some traditional Planet Blech fun?

A loogie-contest judge

A sweat-and-slider

This Spitball Spitter

This rotten egg toss contestant

This Stinky feet contestant

A fart-balloon popper

Go back to Planet Blech and find these things.

Eye gunk salad

Stink-filled chocolates

Slug Stew

Phlegmonade

Toenail casserole

Moldy mucus ad

Go back to the Ship and find these parts of a G.S.S. yechh uniform.

Slime-covered boots

Roach-shaped badge

Fart grenade

Sweat-stained jacket

Moth-chewed hat

Stained pants

Find these gross creatures crawling through the city dump.

Find these sports items hidden in the locker room.

Go back to the science lab and find these things.

A student above the rest

Someone taking a "power nap"

A "de-lighted" student

Something with days that are numbered

A student making a "breakthrough"

Something that is "chalk-full"

Go back to the cafeteria and find these gross food items that were brought from home.

Turkey-and-prune Sandwich

Green-bean muffin

Olive-topped pumpkin pie

Peanut butter and ketchup Sandwich

Chocolate-covered corn

Liver and onions

There are quite a few living things in Chip's room. Can you find some of them?

See if you can find these food items at the party.

Relish-frosted chocolate cake

Feet loaf

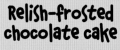

Hot Dog Sundae

Chicken "Potty" Pie

Slug Stew

worm Sandwiches

Stinky Cheese Plate